ASIAPAC COMIC SERIES

Legend of the
MOON MAIDEN

嫦娥奔月

**Illustrated by
Loke Siew Hong**

**Translated by
Koh Kok Kiang**

ASIAPAC • SINGAPORE

Publisher
ASIAPAC BOOKS PTE LTD
629 Aljunied Road #04-06
Cititech Industrial Building
Singapore 389838
Tel: (65) 7453868
Fax: (65) 7453822
Email apacbks@singnet.com.sg

Visit us at our Internet home page
http://www.span.com.au/asiapac.htm

First published September 1996

©1996 ASIAPAC BOOKS, SINGAPORE
ISBN 981-3068-47-7

Cover illustration by Loke Siew Hong
Cover design by Marked Point Design
Body text in 8/9 pt Helvetica
Printed in Singapore by
Kin Keong Printing

Publisher's Note

As a publisher dedicated to the promotion of works on Chinese culture, we are pleased to bring you this graphic presentation of *Moon Maiden*. *Moon Maiden* is a famous fable about how the goddess Chang-e came to live on the moon. When the Chinese admire the beauty of the moon while enjoying mooncakes during the Mid-Autumn Festival (*Zhongqiu Jie*), also known as Mooncake Festival, they often recall this story. Indeed, so popular is this legend that many mooncake brands are named after Chang-e and the containers often have a picture showing her soaring to the moon.

There are many versions of the tale of how Chang-e became an immortal in the Palace of the Moon. This comic version depicts Chang-e and Hou Yi as admirable characters devoted to each other. The story begins with a chance meeting between Chang-e and Hou Yi that leads to romance, and ends with Chang-e flying to the moon. This romantic plot is made more intriguing by the comic illustrations provided by Malaysian artist Loke Siew Hong.

We would like to take this opportunity to thank Loke Siew Hong for his lively comic illustrations. Our appreciation, too, to Koh Kok Kiang for translating this volume and writing the Introduction, and the production team for putting in their best effort in the publication of this book.

Introduction

Moon Maiden is a famous fable about how the goddess Chang-e came to live on the moon. The fable originated during the Tang Dynasty (AD 618 to 907) and there are several versions of the tale of how Chang-e became associated with the moon. Some versions say she was good and some say she was bad.

According to the versions that Chang-e was a flawed character, her curiosity got the better of her and she stole the pill of immortality which the Queen Mother of the West gave to her husband, the Divine Archer Hou Yi.

Hou Yi had been told that he could not eat the pill immediately but had to purify himself through praying and fasting for 12 months. He thus hid the pill in the house. One day, however, he had to leave home to take up an urgent assignment.

During his absence, his wife Chang-e noticed a soft light and a sweet fragrance emanating from a room and she found the pill of immortality. As soon as she popped it into her mouth, the law of gravity lost its power over her and she could fly at will. Shortly, her husband returned and upon hearing his footsteps, she hastily flew out of the window.

Hou Yi pursued her but a strong gust of wind sent him tumbling back to earth. Chang-e flew all the way to the moon but she was panting so hard that she spat out the pill casing, which transformed into a jade rabbit. Chang-e herself turned into a three-legged toad.

Hou Yi was sent to live in a palace in the sun and the couple was able to meet on the fifteenth of every month when the moon is at its brightest. Chang-e and Hou Yi, symbolising the moon and the sun respectively, have come to be regarded as representing yin and yang, feminine and masculine, dark and light, positive and negative - the duality that governs the universe.

Versions of the story that depict Chang-e as good say that her husband was a powerful but cruel person and she flew to her moon to get away from him.

The traditional version of the story of Chang-e and Hou Yi is as follows:

The legendary Emperor Yao, in the twelfth year of his reign (2346 BC), was walking in the streets of his capital Huaiyang one day when he met a man carrying a bow and arrows, his bow being bound with a piece of red stuff.

This man was Chijiang Ziyu. He told the emperor he was a skillful archer and could ride the wind.

To test his skill, Yao ordered him to shoot one of his arrows at a pine tree on the top of a mountain nearby. The archer's arrow struck the tree and he jumped on a current of air to retrieve it. Because of this the emperor bestowed on him the title of the Divine Archer.

At this time terrible calamities began to lay waste the land. Ten suns - nine of them false - appeared in the sky and the heat scorched all crops and the land became parched. Monsters were also causing havoc. Hou Yi was entrusted with the task of eliminating the scourge, which he did.

Later, Hou Yi met the Queen Mother of the West and asked her for a pill of immortality. Hearing that he was a good architect, she asked him to build her a palace which he duly accomplished. She gave him the coveted pill which would make him immortal as well as able to fly at will.

Hou Yi was told that he could not eat the pill immediately. Instead, he had to go through a twelve-month preparatory course of exercise and diet, without which the pill would not produce the desired results.

On reaching home, the archer hid his precious pill under a rafter, lest anyone should steal it, and then began his preparatory course.

However, a strange man named Chisel-Tooth, who had round eyes and a long projecting tooth, was sowing terror in the south and Hou Yi was summoned to deal with him. One arrow was all that Hou Yi needed to finish him off.

During Hou Yi's absence, Chang-e saw a white light which seemed to issue from a beam in the roof while a most savoury smell filled every room. With the aid of a ladder, she reached the source of the light and found the pill of immortality.

She swallowed it and suddenly found herself freed from the laws of gravity and was about to go on her first flight when Hou Yi returned. He went to look for the pill and, not finding it, questioned Chang-e about the matter.

Chang-e, seized with fear, opened a window and flew out. Hou Yi took his bow and arrows and pursued her. The moon was full, the night clear, and he saw Chang-e soar rapidly in front of him. Just when he was quickening his pace to catch up with her, a blast of wind struck him to the ground like a dried twig.

Chang-e continued her flight until she arrived on the moon. All of a sudden she began to cough and vomited the coating of the pill of immortality, which was changed into a rabbit as white as the purest jade. Chang-e decided to live there. She was said to have been transformed into a toad, whose outline was visible on the surface of the moon.

The God of the Immortals told Hou Yi not to be annoyed with Chang-e, saying that everyone's fate was predestined. He said that Chang-e, through having borrowed the forces which by right belonged to Hou Yi, had become an immortal in the Palace of the Moon. As for Hou Yi, he deserved much for having so bravely fought the nine false suns. As a reward, he was made an immortal to guard the Palace of the Sun. Thus the yin and the yang would be reunited.

Hou Yi went to meet Chang-e on the moon and from that time onwards, on the fifteenth day of every month, he would visit her in her palace. This is the conjunction of the yang and yin, male and female principles, which causes the greatest brilliance of the moon during that time.

Kok Kok Kiang

CONTENTS

Chance Meeting That Leads To Romance

邂逅—情根暗種

2

Legend has it that a long time ago there
was a young goddess who was fond of
sneaking into the human world for tours.
She also used her supernatural powers
to help the people she encountered.

Ouch!

Huff!

Puff!

Old lady,
why are you
in such a
hurry?

The weather is so hot. You must be thirsty. Why not drink some of my water and rest for a while?

Thank you! Gulp!!

Young lady, are you also going to town?

6

Thank you!
I'm Chang-e.
Goodbye!

Goodbye!

The moon is dazzling. I wonder what the surface of the moon is like.

10

Swoosh!

12

13

15

North of the Yellow River.

Your lordship, Emperor Yao has a task for you.

Eh?

Strange beasts have appeared in the western regions and in the Kunlun mountains of the Central Plain. Emperor Yao wants you to go there immediately to eliminate the evil.

I'll obey the edict.

Chang-e, when I have accomplished my mission, I will definitely go to the north of the Yellow River to look for you.

Slaying Monster With One Divine Stroke
除魔—初顯神威

Kunlun mountains

Oh!!

Fire!

22

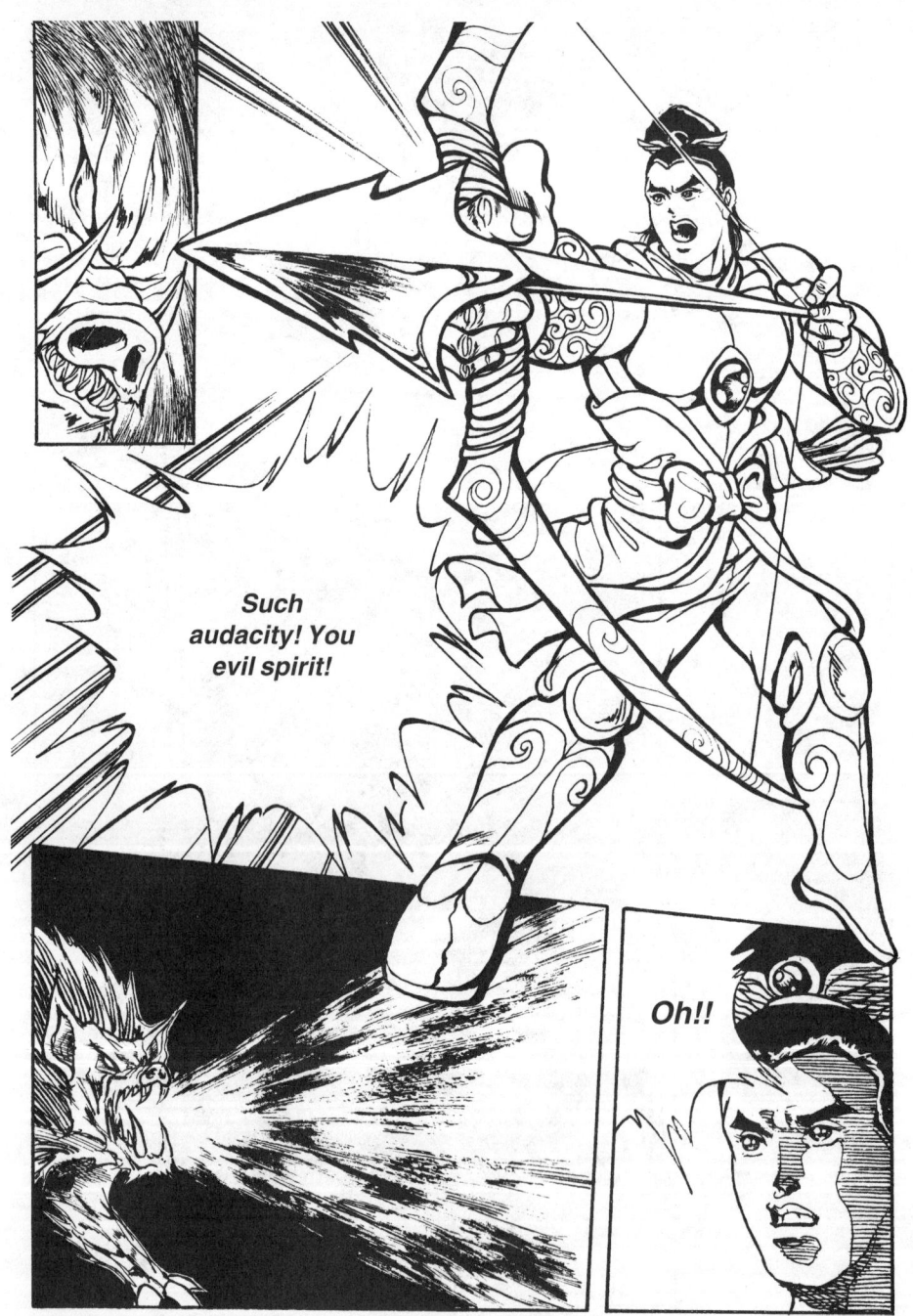

Such audacity! You evil spirit!

Oh!!

24

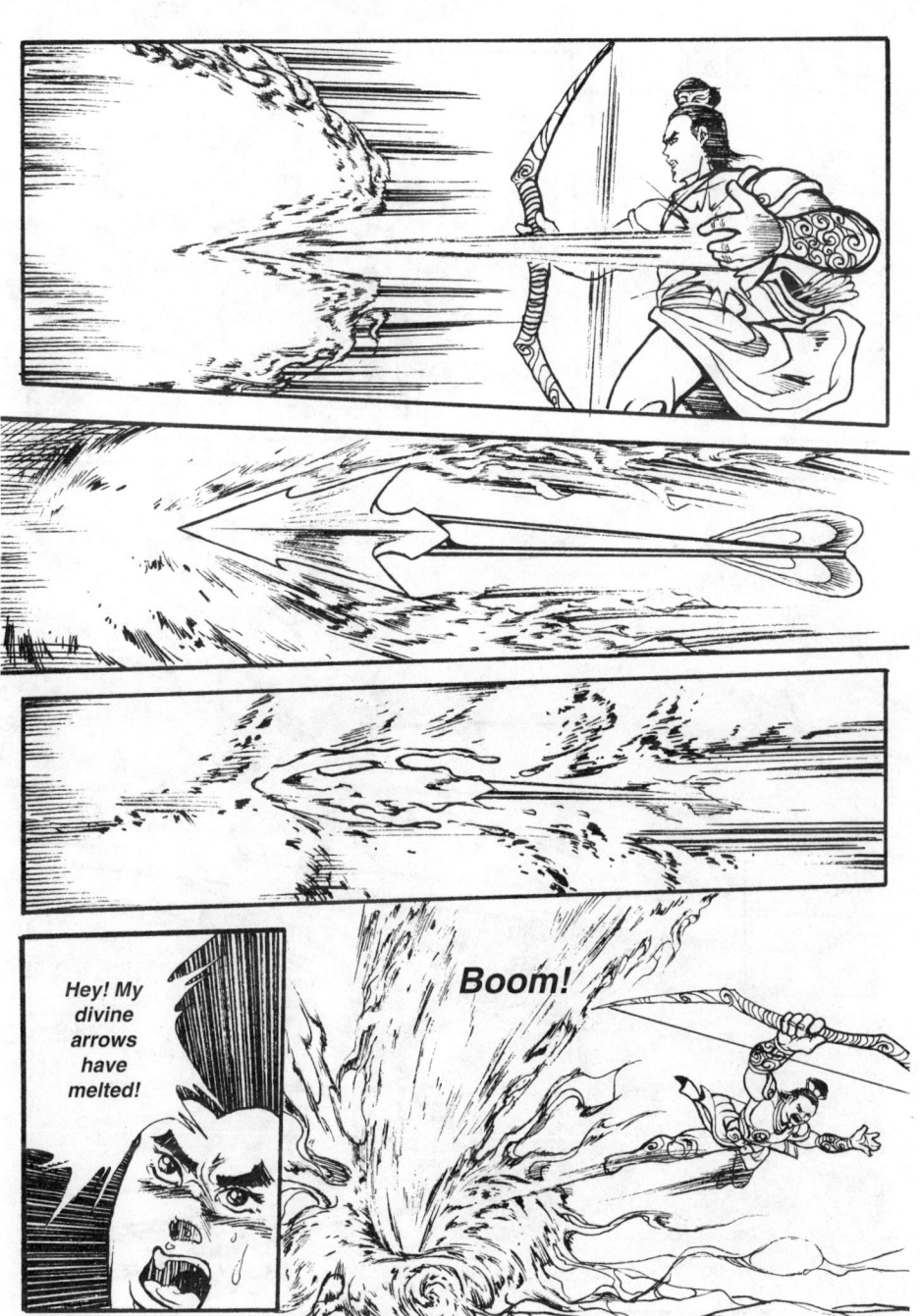

Wow, what a formidable beast!

Watch my continuous archery!

GRRRRR!

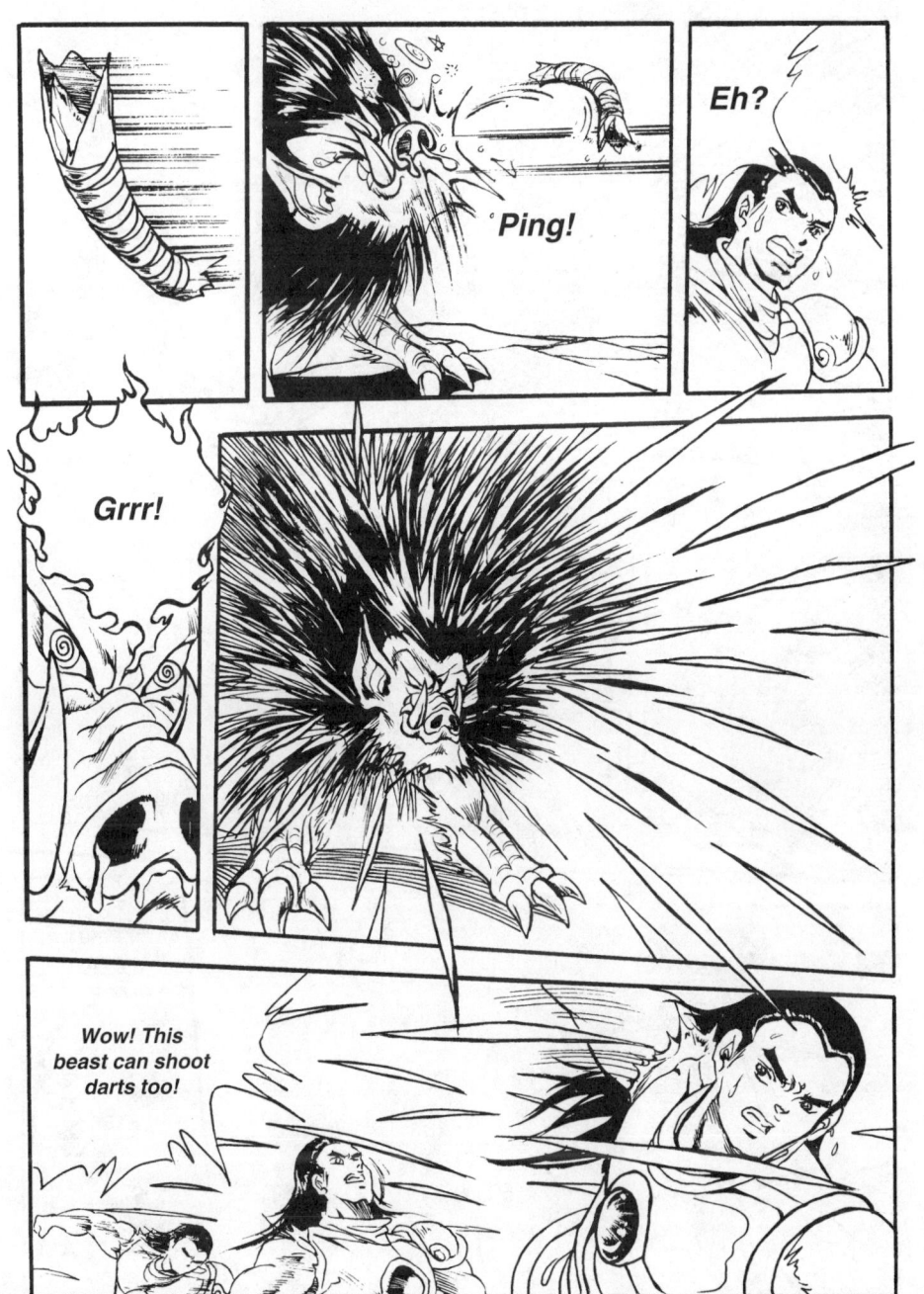

29

30

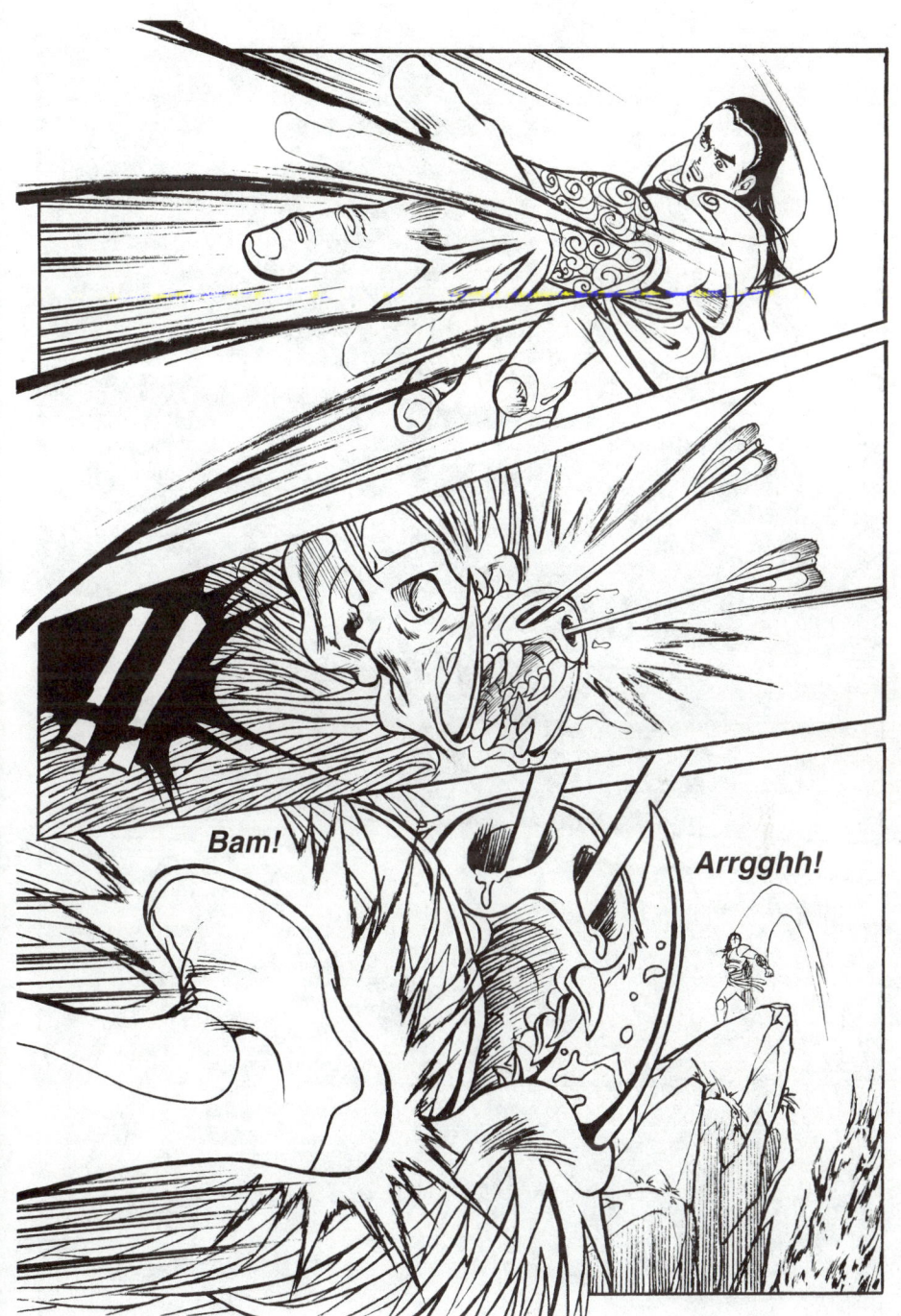

Finally
it is
finished!

Now that I have eliminated the monster boar, I'm going to the western region to deal with the wind spirit.

Stone Mountain in the Western Region.

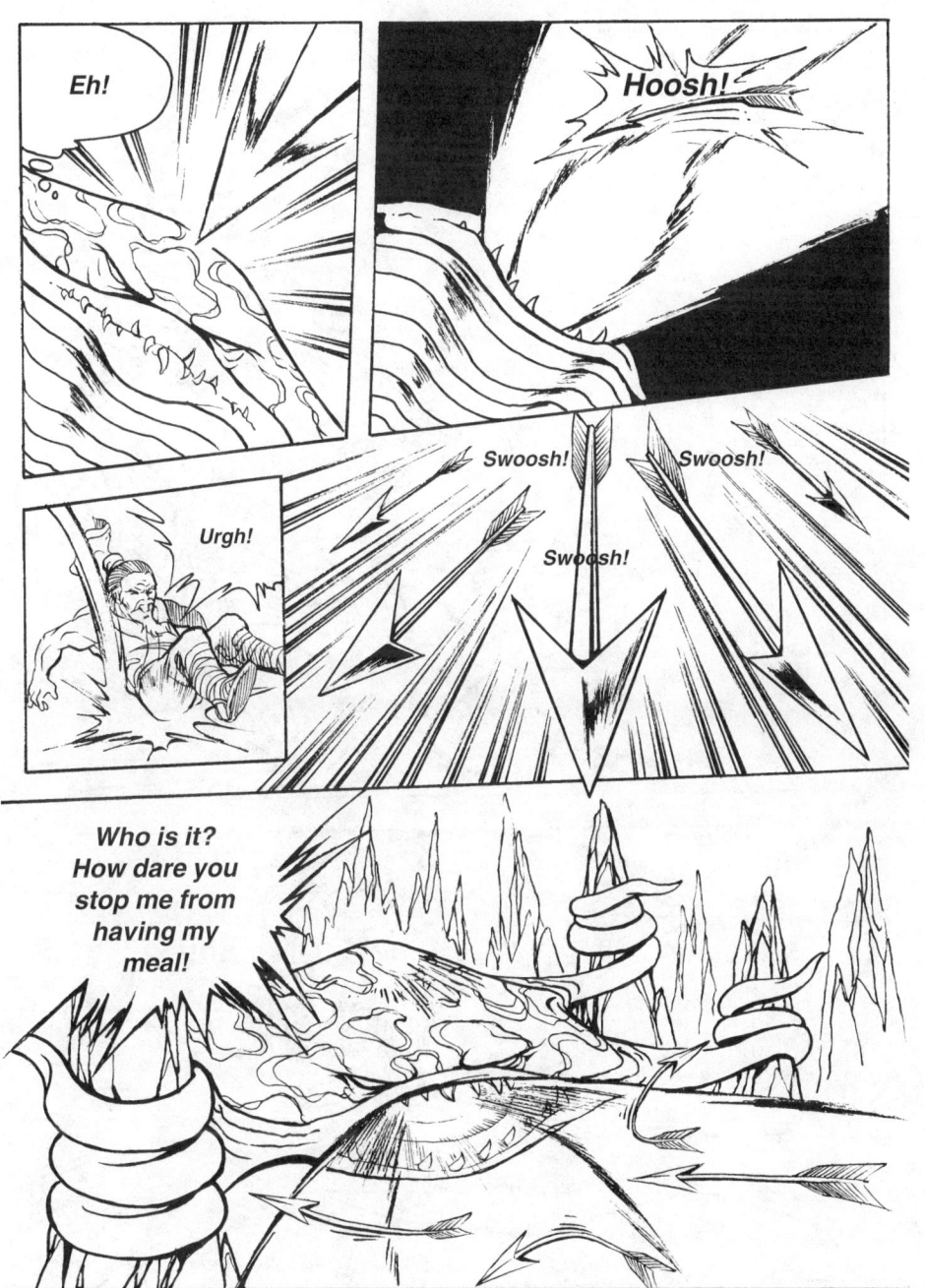

35

36

Yuks! Since you are able to swallow people in one gulp, I believe you must have eaten many people.

So what? I, the Wind Spirit, will make a meal of the Divine Archer as well.

Whoosh!

Watch my prowess!

Wah!

37

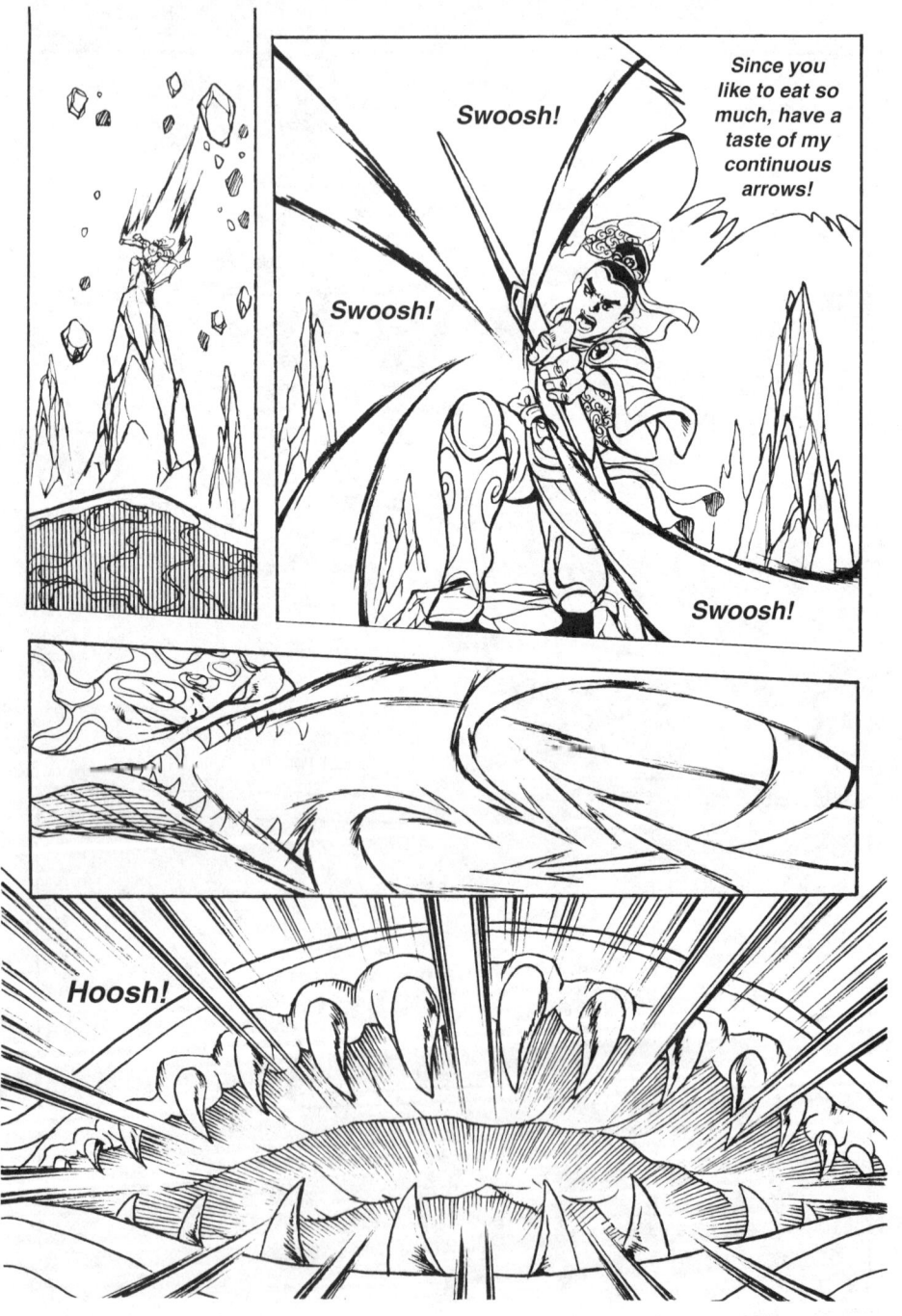

Wah!!

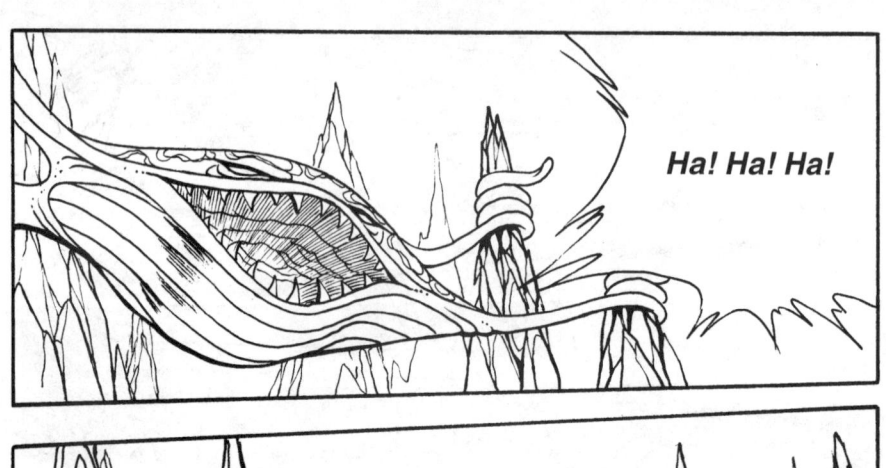

Ha! Ha! Ha!

Eh!

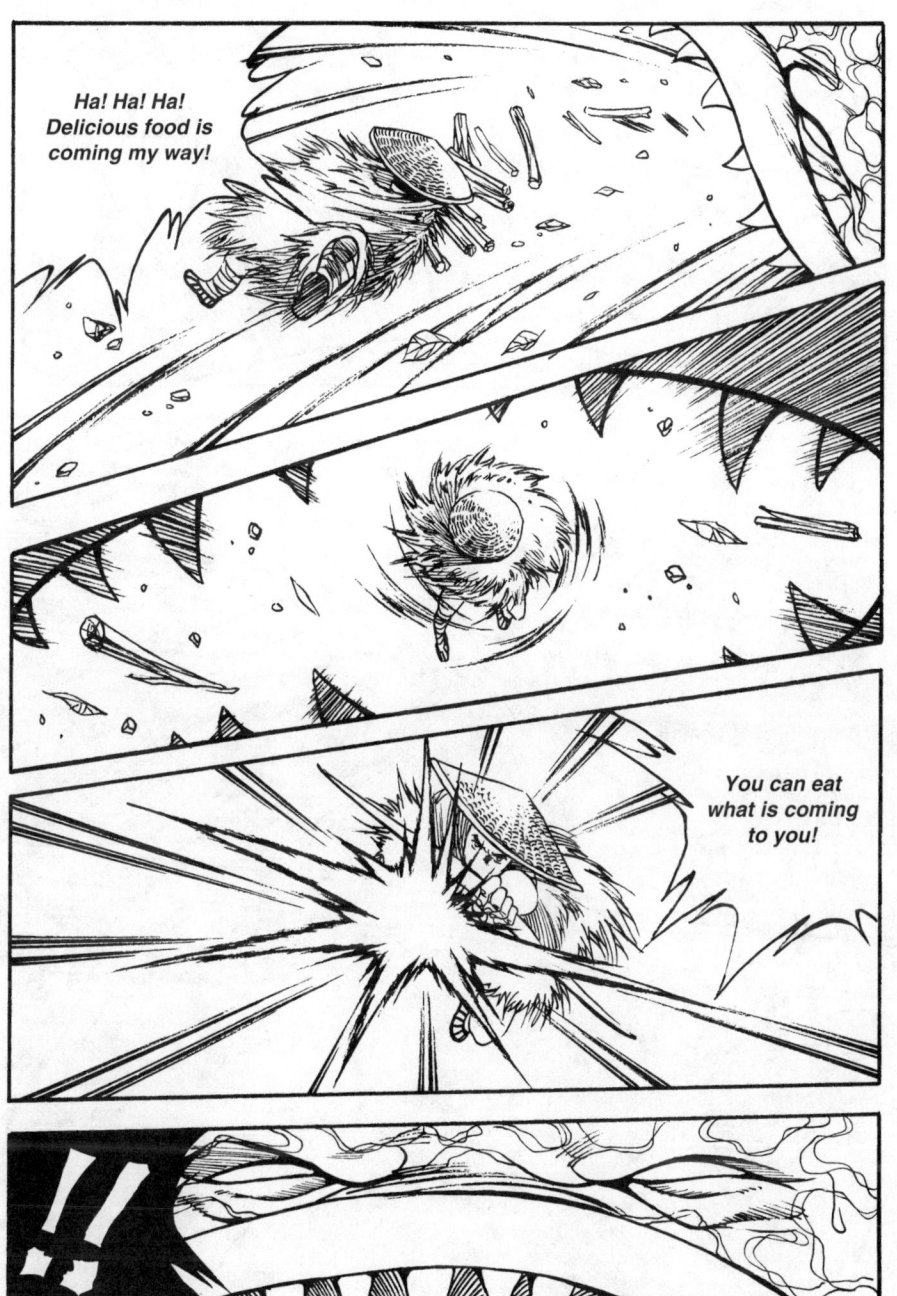

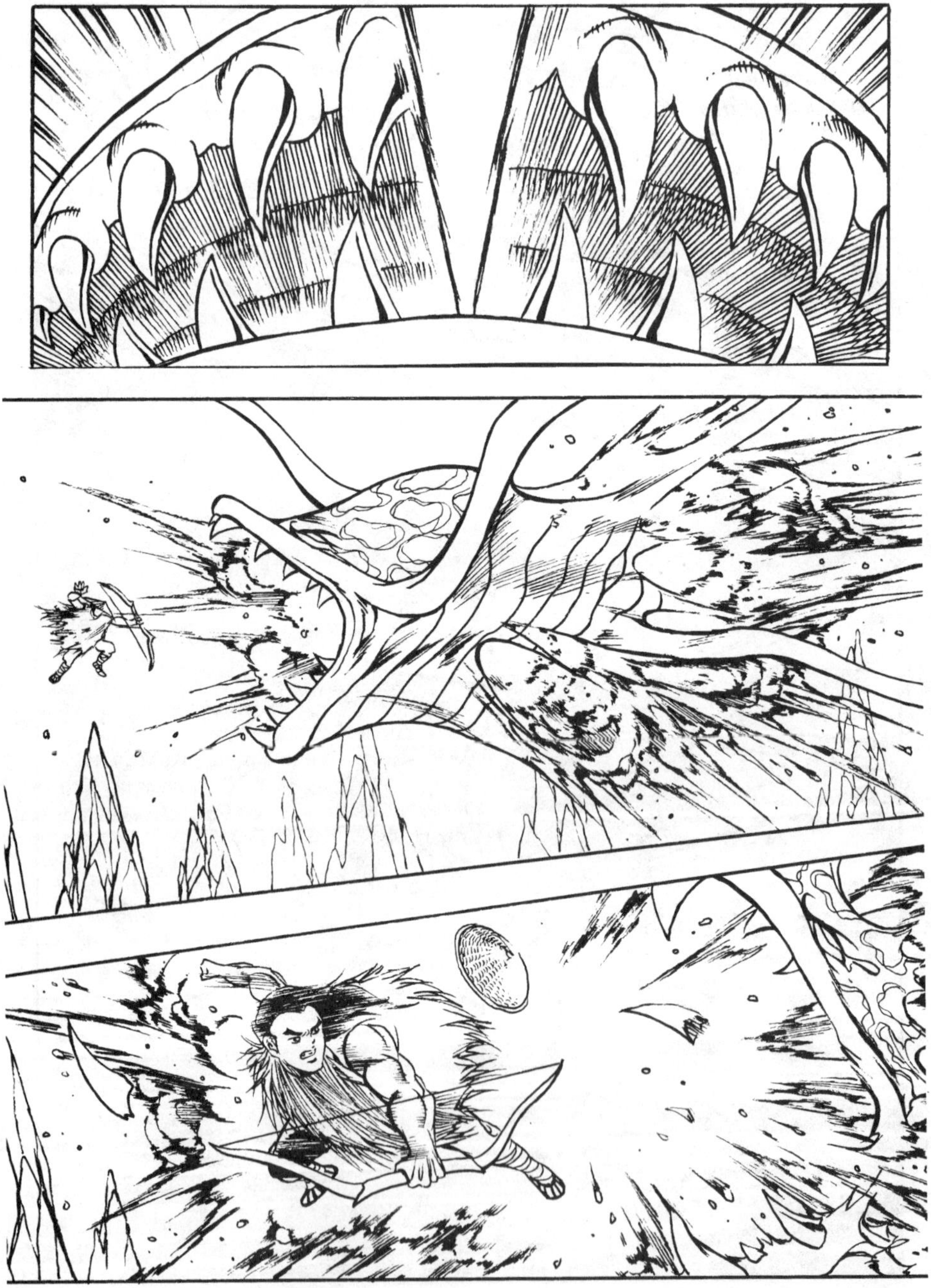

43

A Match Decided After A Reunion
相會—緣定今生

North of the Yellow River

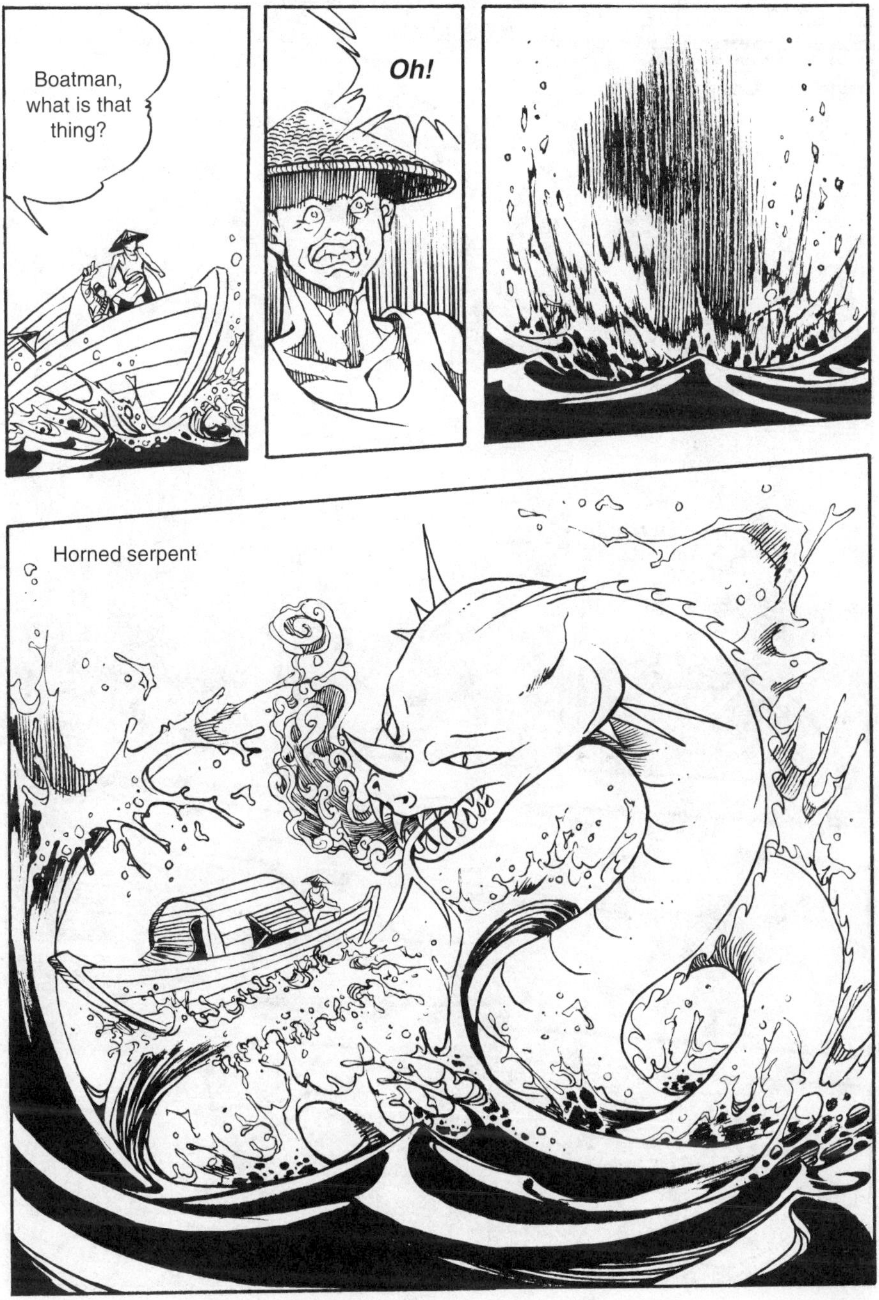

Boatman, what is that thing?

Oh!

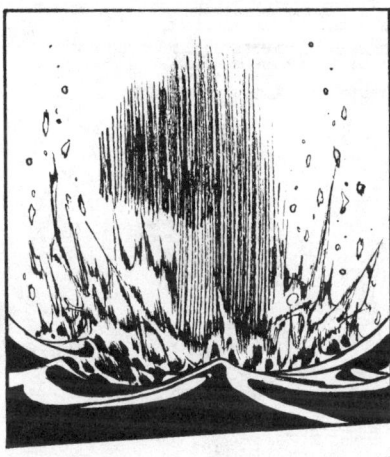

Horned serpent

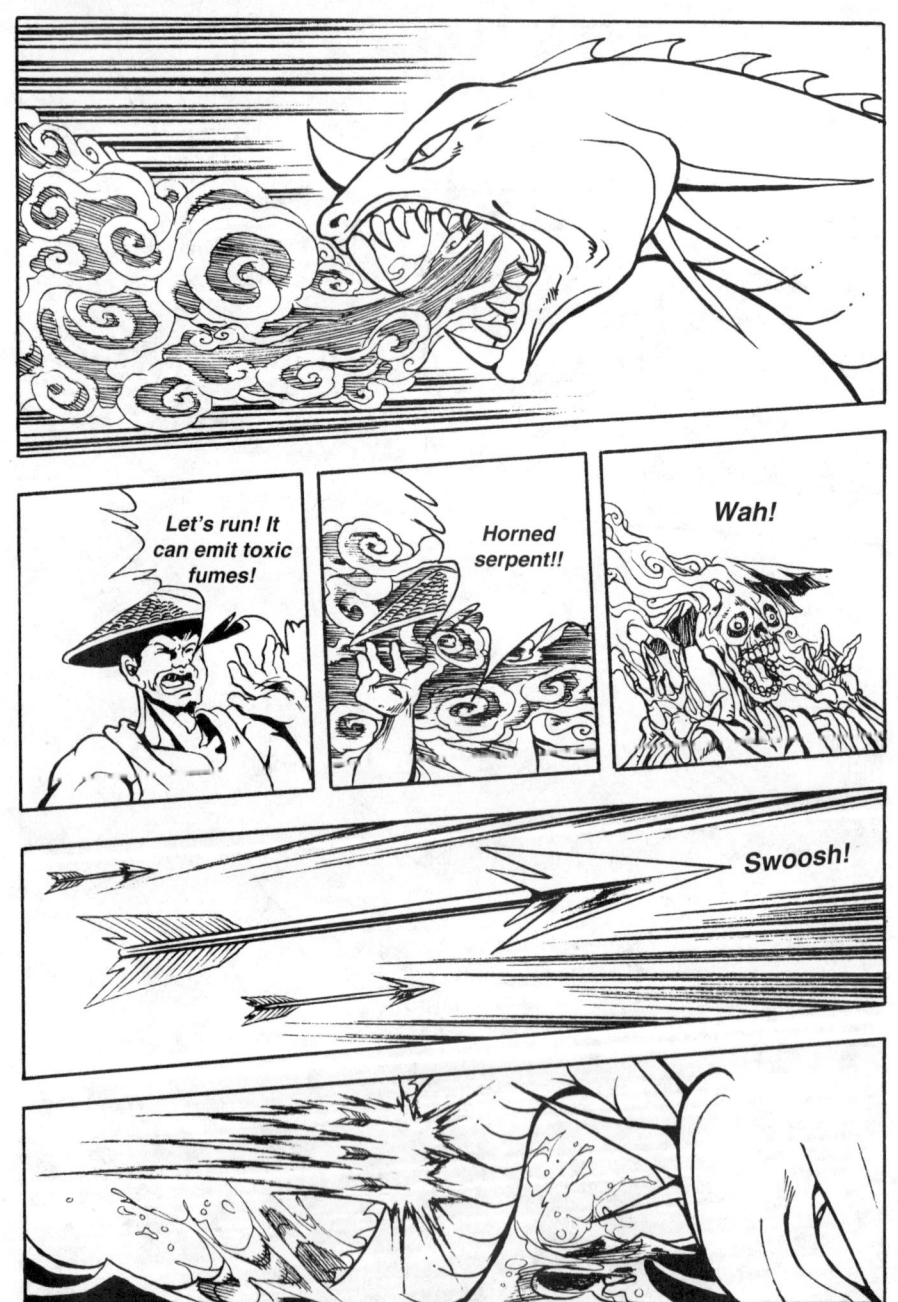

49

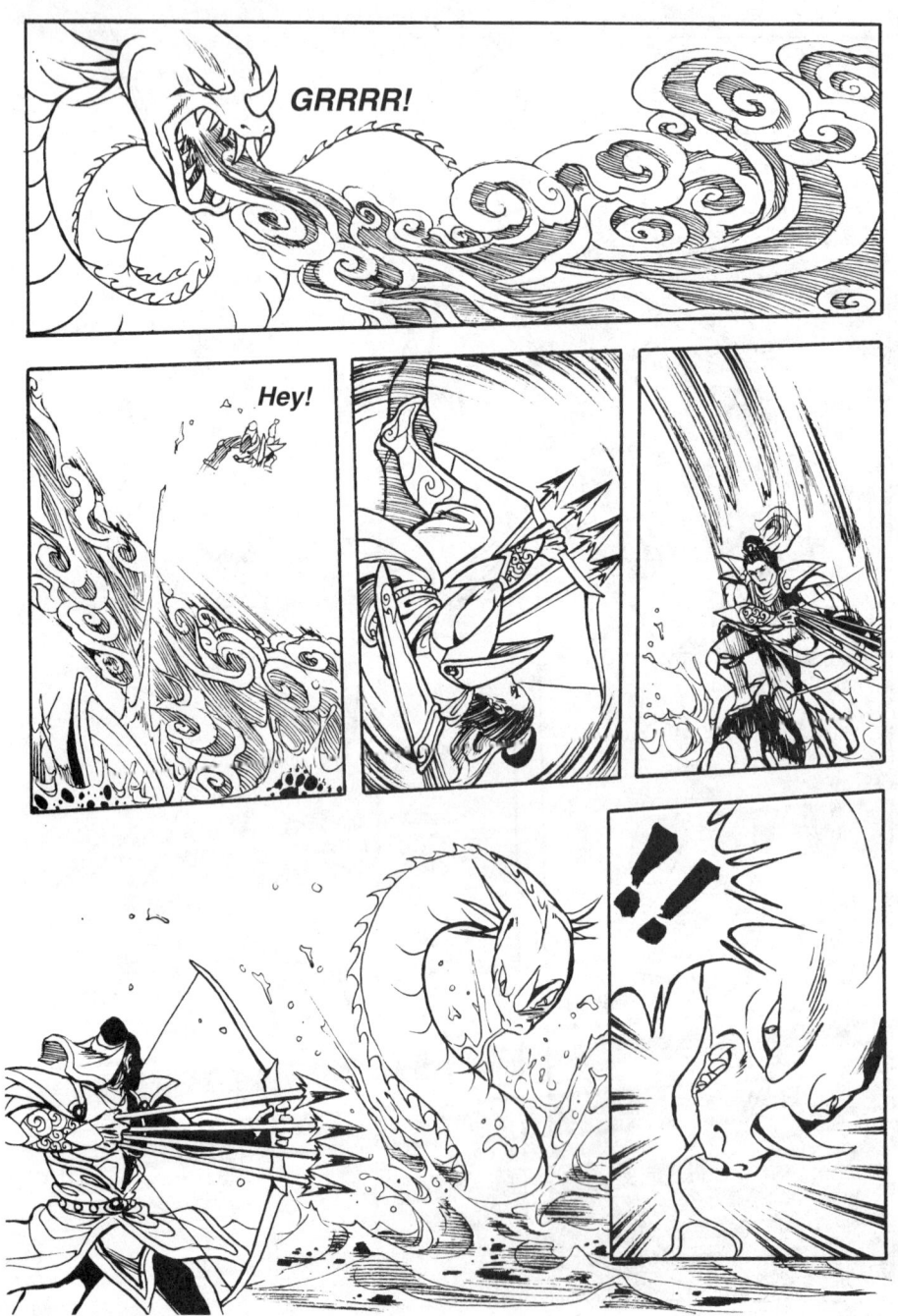

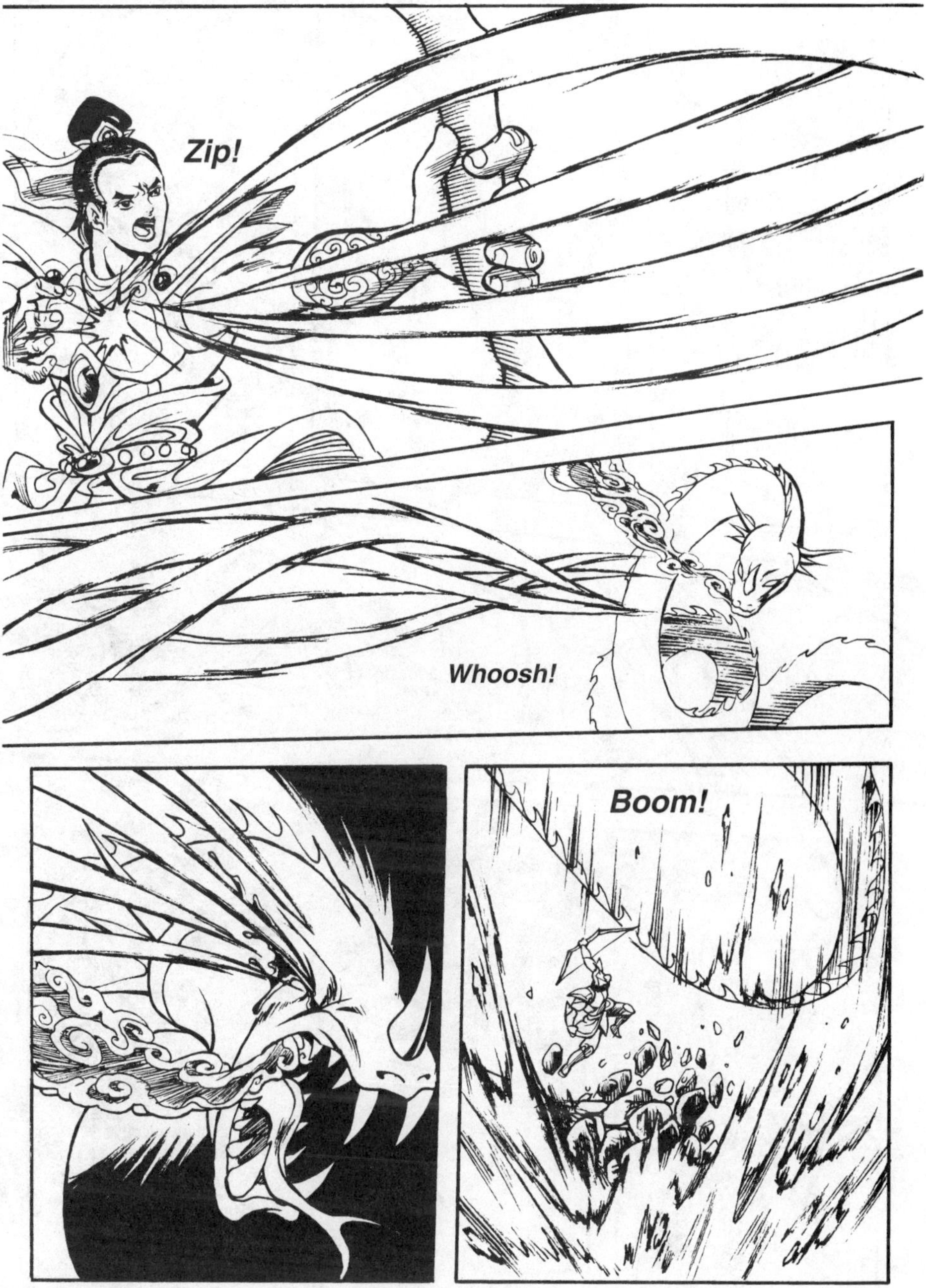

Zip!

Whoosh!

Boom!

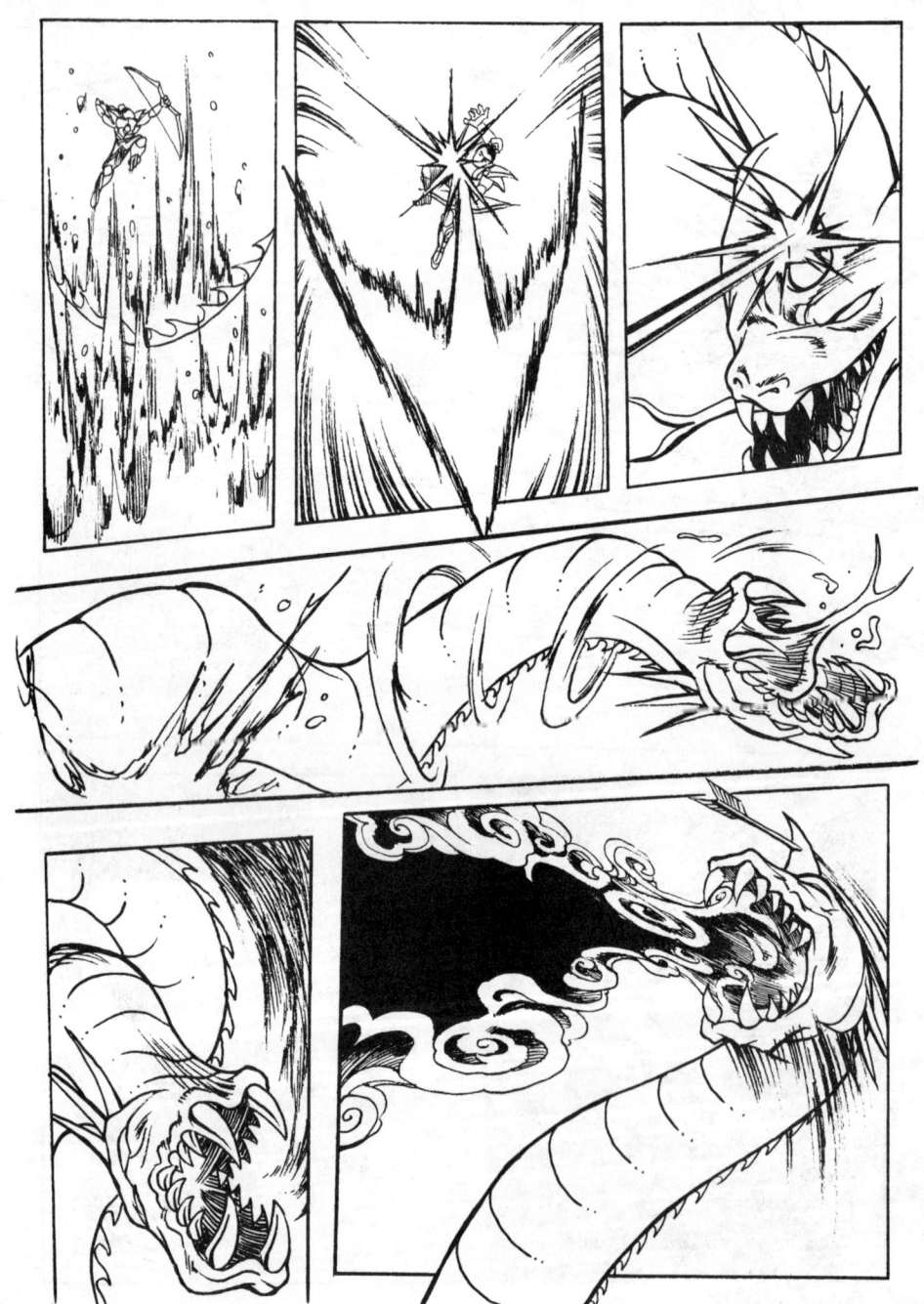

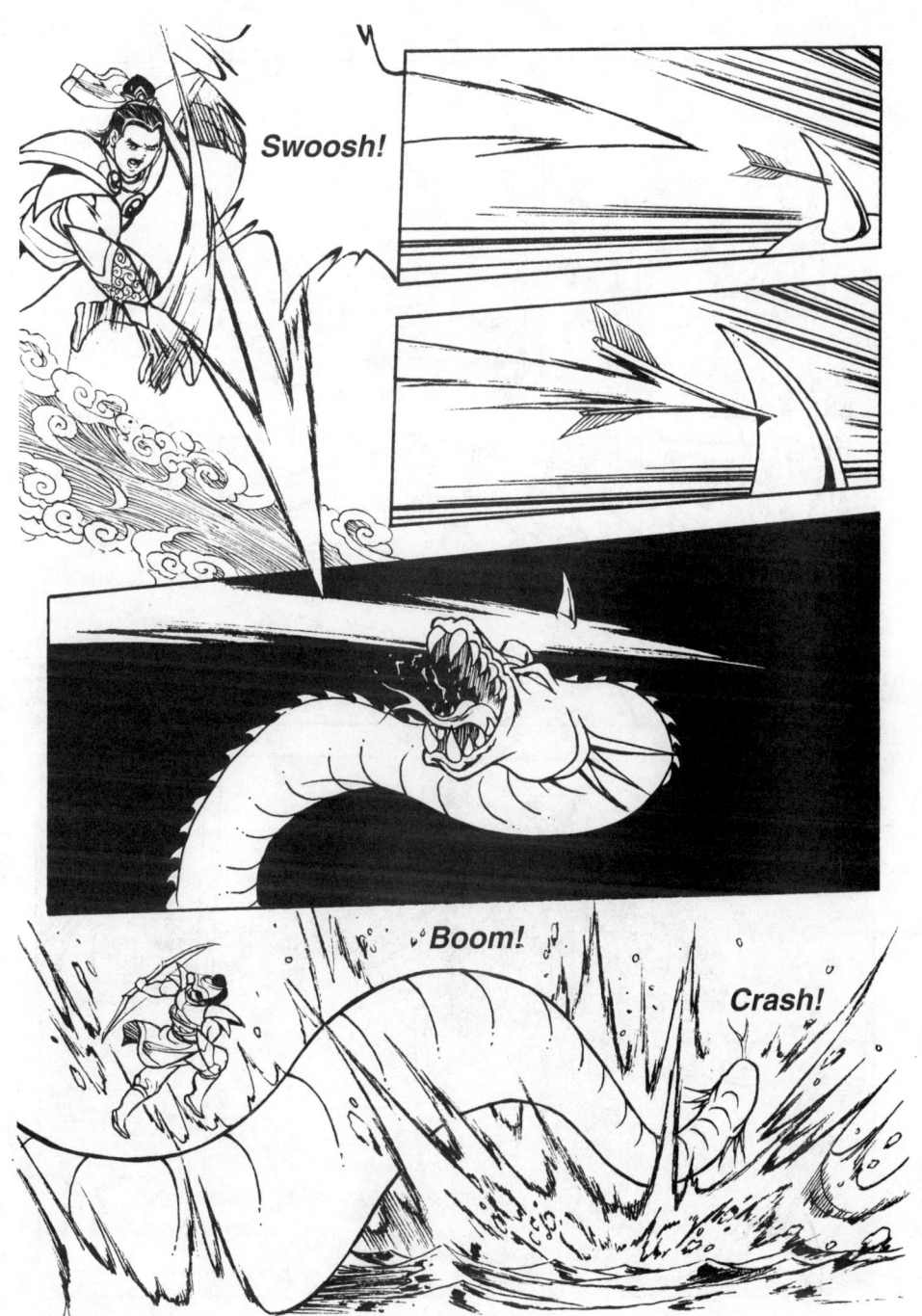

Is the monster still there?

Oh, no! It's not a monster!

54

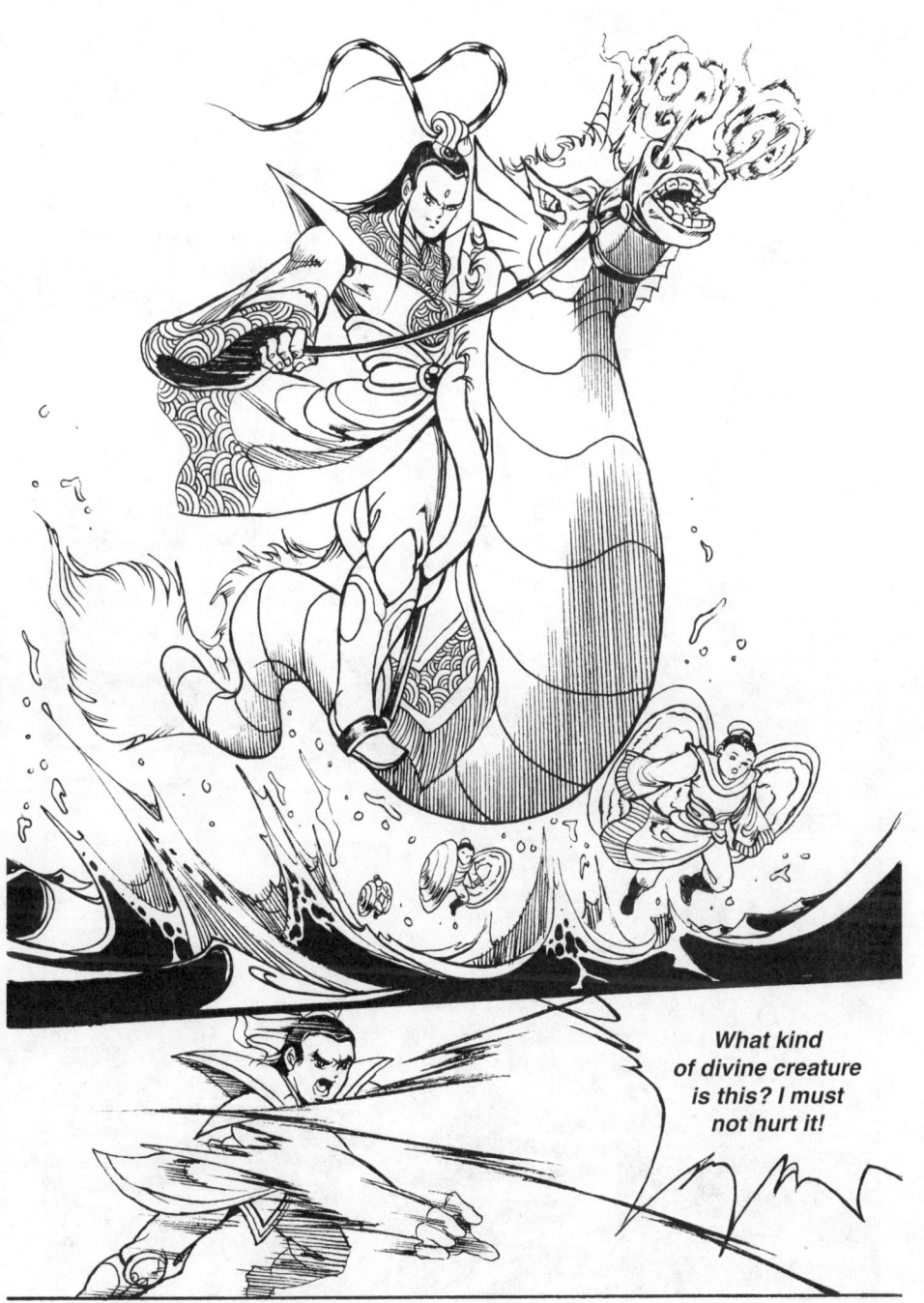

55

56

Chang-e?

58

Chang-e, are you willing to be my wife?

Wonderful! Emperor Yao will be very happy to meet you!

Eh! What is that?

Hak!

How come there are ten suns in the sky?

Eliminating The Nine Evil Suns

射日 — 后羿射日

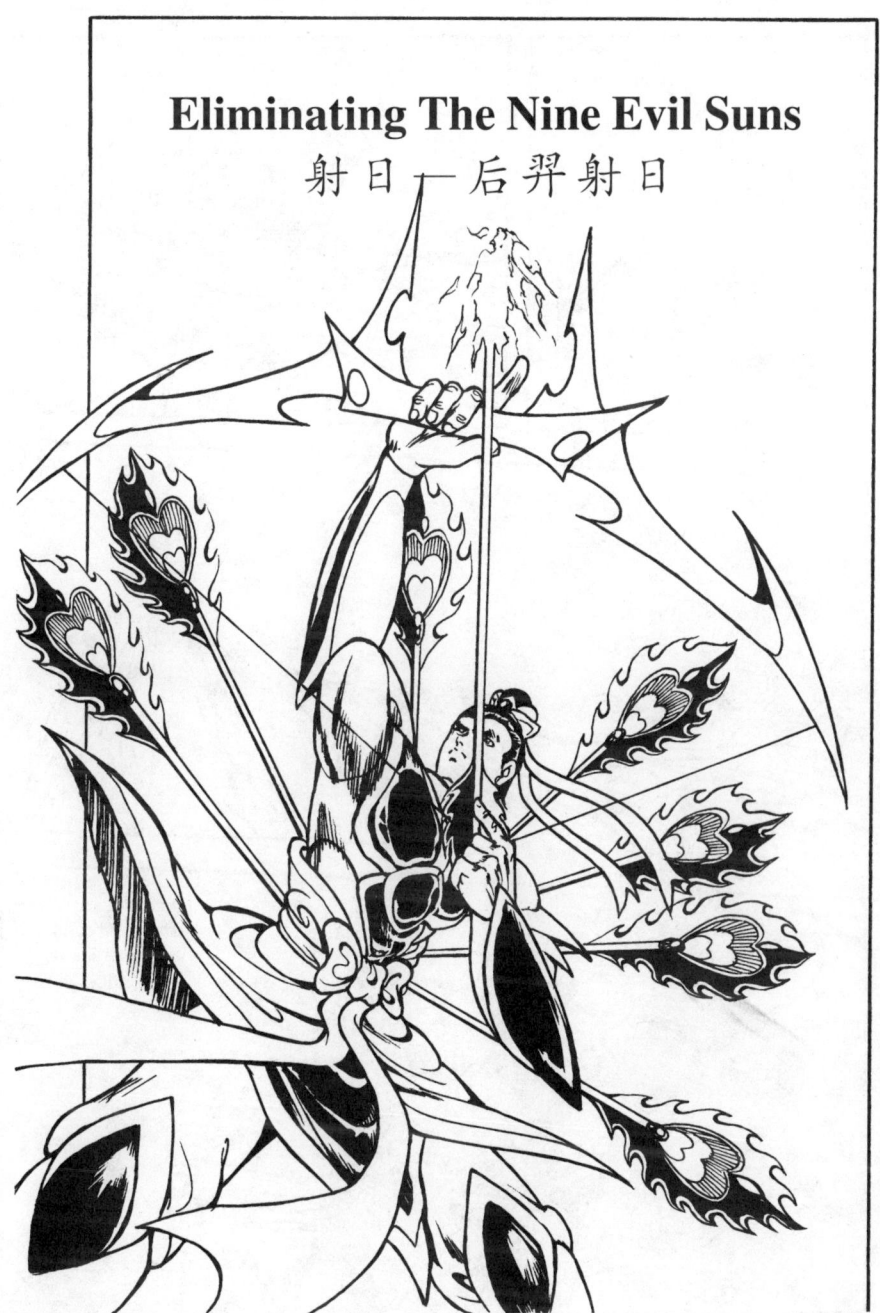

It has been like this for more than a month.

The earth has become like a furnace.

68

No!

I cannot admit defeat!

Huh!

Eh! How come I'm unharmed?

70

Water!
I need some
water!

Great old
man, you can
have some
water!

Really?
Thanks!

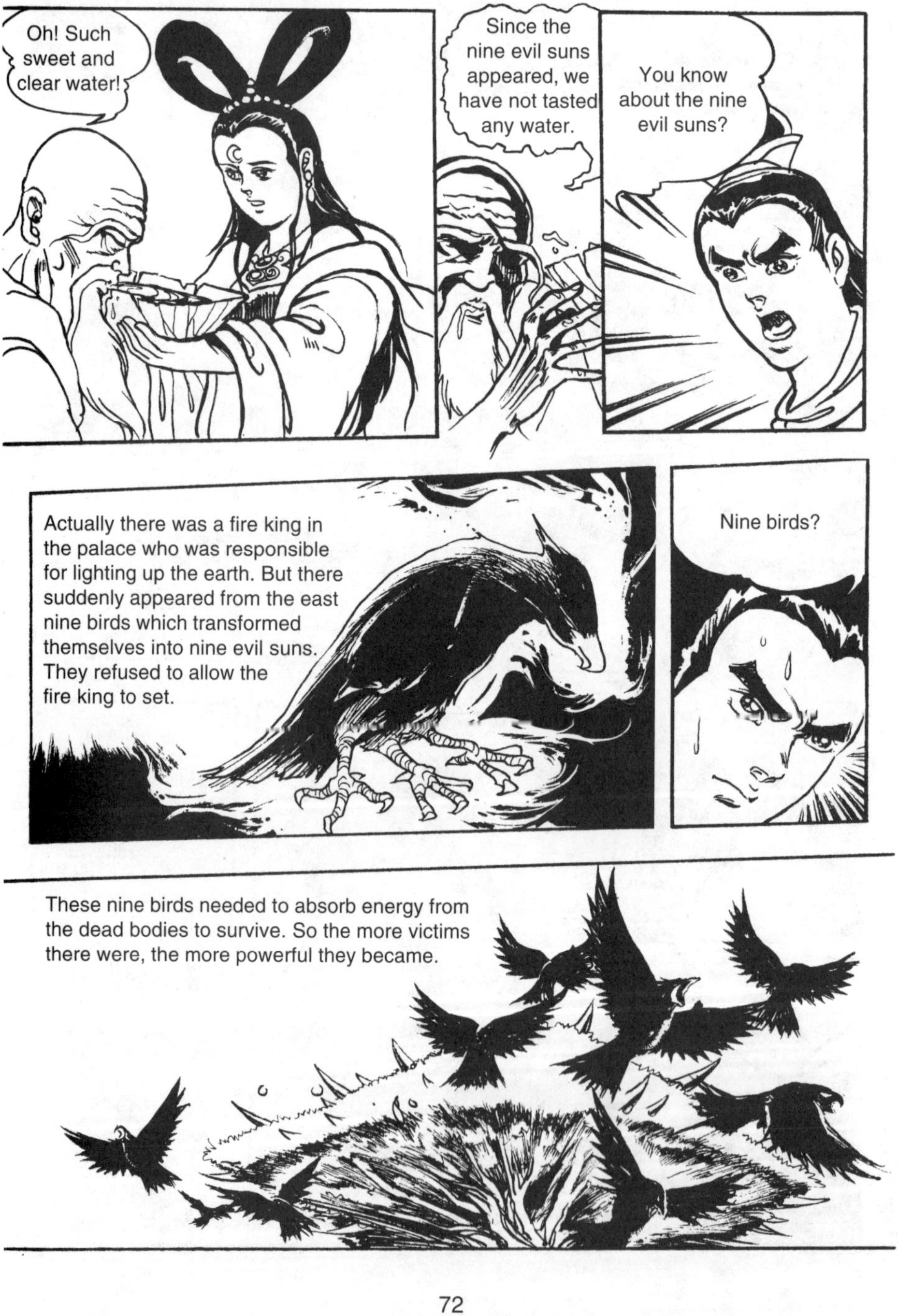

Oh! Such sweet and clear water!

Since the nine evil suns appeared, we have not tasted any water.

You know about the nine evil suns?

Actually there was a fire king in the palace who was responsible for lighting up the earth. But there suddenly appeared from the east nine birds which transformed themselves into nine evil suns. They refused to allow the fire king to set.

Nine birds?

These nine birds needed to absorb energy from the dead bodies to survive. So the more victims there were, the more powerful they became.

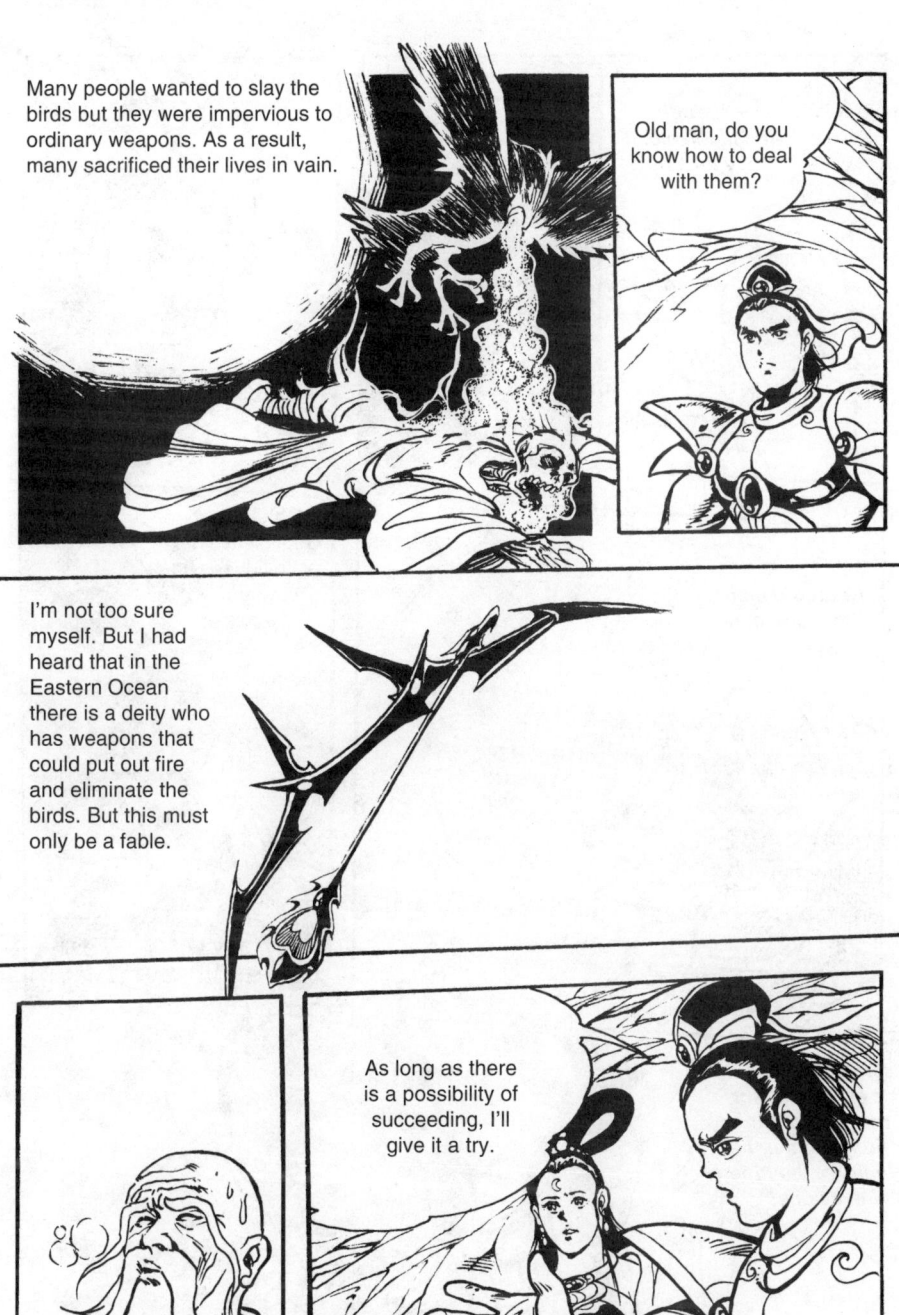

Many people wanted to slay the birds but they were impervious to ordinary weapons. As a result, many sacrificed their lives in vain.

Old man, do you know how to deal with them?

I'm not too sure myself. But I had heard that in the Eastern Ocean there is a deity who has weapons that could put out fire and eliminate the birds. But this must only be a fable.

As long as there is a possibility of succeeding, I'll give it a try.

73

Although this is a fable, it may turn out to be true!

You ... You ... Go ... Quickly, go ...

Yes!

Great old man! Great old man!!

Oh! Almighty God, please help us to find the fire bow and fire arrows!

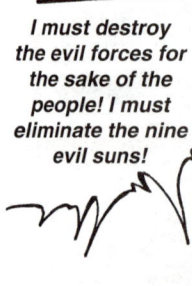

I must destroy the evil forces for the sake of the people! I must eliminate the nine evil suns!

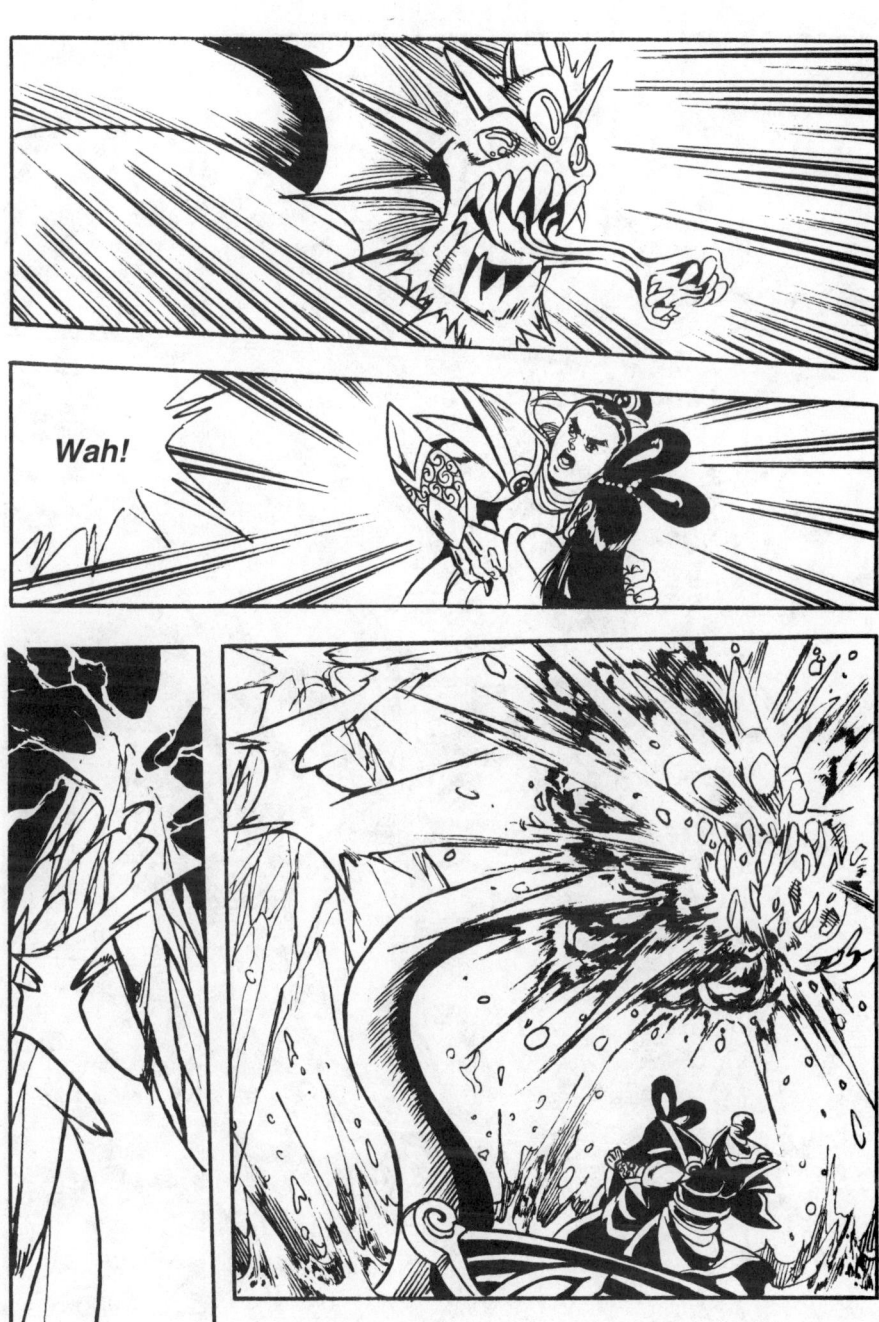

Wah!

78

79

81

Zap! Bang!

Swoosh!

Urgh!

Boom!

**Flight To The Moon
And Eternal Longing**
奔月—永恒相思

The centipede looks dead but has not become stiff. But if it goes on like this even if it pretends to be dead it would eventually die.

As long as it does not harm people, every creature has a right to live.

Just as I thought, Hou Yi, you are a kind-hearted person.

Come with me. I am the royal dragon that will show you the way.

You have passed the test. Just in front of you is Mount Shu.

Remember, only those who are compassionate, wise and courageous have the privilege of meeting the Queen Mother of the West.

Thank you for your guidance.

Is this Mount Shu of the West?

Hou Yi, you have seen Mount Shu, but you must overcome this obstacle before you can ascend the mountain.

What!

No, the distance is too great. There is no way one can leap across.

Well, it is up to your courage to find out if Mount Shu can be reached.

Queen Mother, if I can't save Chang-e, I won't want to drag out my existence on earth.

Hou Yi, I know what you are here for.

Please grant me my wish, Queen Mother of the West.

Here are two pills of immortality, one each for you and Chang-e. But finally, everything depends on your spiritual will and affinity.

Thanks, Queen Mother of the West!

Why? How come she is not showing any response?

Look, the moon is so big and round!

It is becoming brighter.

Chang-e, I shall think about you always.

Hou Yi, don't be sad. This is all predestined.

Queen Mother of the West!

103

Thus, Hou Yi and Chang-e came to be associated with the sun and the moon. The only pity is that the sun and the moon cannot meet. Hou Yi and Chang-e can only take turns day after day and year after year to bring light to the human world.

Latest Titles in
Strategy & Leadership Series

Chinese Business Strategies

The Chinese are known for being shrewd businessmen able to thrive under the toughest market conditions. The secret of their success lies in 10 time-tested principles of Chinese entrepreneurship.

This book offers readers 30 real-life, ancient case studies with comments on their application in the context of modern business.

Sixteen Strategies of Zhuge Liang

Zhuge Liang, the legendary statesman and military commander during the Three Kingdoms Period, is the epitome of wisdom.

Well-grounded in military principles of Sun Zi and other masters before him, he excelled in applying them in state administration and his own innovations, thus winning many spectacular victories with his uncanny anticipation of enemy moves.

Strategy & Leadership Series by Wang Xuanming

Thirty-six Stratagems: Secret Art of War
Translated by Koh Kok Kiang (cartoons) &
Liu Yi (text of the stratagems)
A Chinese military classic which emphasizes deceptive schemes to achieve military objectives. It has attracted the attention of military authorities and general readers alike.

Six Strategies for War: The Practice of Effective Leadership
Translated by Alan Chong
A powerful book for rulers, administrators and leaders, it covers critical areas in management and warfare including: how to recruit talents and manage the state; how to beat the enemy and build an empire; how to lead wisely; and how to manoeuvre brilliantly.

Gems of Chinese Wisdom: Mastering the Art of Leadership
Translated by Leong Weng Kam
Wise up with this delightful collection of tales and anecdotes on the wisdom of great men and women in Chinese history, including Confucius, Meng Changjun and Gou Jian.

Three Strategies of Huang Shi Gong: The Art of Government
Translated by Alan Chong
Reputedly one of man's oldest monograph on military strategy, it unmasks the secrets behind brilliant military manoeuvres, clever deployment and control of subordinates, and effective government.

100 Strategies of War: Brilliant Tactics in Action
Translated by Yeo Ai Hoon
The book captures the essence of extensive military knowledge and practice, and explores the use of psychology in warfare, the importance of building diplomatic relations with the enemy's neighbours, the use of espionage and reconnaissance, etc.

SPECIAL OFFER

Strategy & Leadership Series

- [ ] Chinese Business Strategies
- [ ] Three Strategies of Huang Shi Gong
- [ ] Six Strategies for War
- [ ] Sixteen Strategies of Zhuge Liang
- [ ] Thirty-six Stratagems
- [ ] 100 Strategies of War
- [ ] Gems of Chinese Wisdom

Make your subscription for any 5 volumes or more of this comic series (tick box) and enjoy **20% discount**.

Original Price: S$15.90 per volume (*exclusive* of GST)

Offer at special discount (*Inclusive of* postage):-

	5 Volumes	6 Volumes	7 Volumes
Singapore	68.30	82.20	95.30
Malaysia	71.60	88.30	101.00
International-by sea mail	78.60	100.30	113.00

* All Prices in Singapore Dollars. 3% GST charge for local orders.

I wish to subscribe for the above-mentioned titles

at the nett price of **S$** _____ (*inclusive of* postage)

- [ ] **For Singapore orders only:**
  Enclosed is my postal order/money order/cheque/ for **S$** _____

  (No.: _____)

- [ ] **For Singapore/Malaysia/International orders:**
  Credit card. Please charge the amount of SIN$ _____ to my credit card

VISA [ ]   Card No. _____ Card Holder's Name _____

MASTER [ ]   Expiry Date _____ Order Date _____ Signature _____

Name _____

Address _____

_____ **Tel** _____

Send to: ASIAPAC BOOKS PTE LTD 629 Aljunied Road #04-06 Cititech Industrial Building
Singapore 389838 Tel: 65 -7453868 Fax: 65 -7453822

Note:
For this offer of 20% discount, there is no restriction on the titles ordered, that is, you may order any 5 or more of the series. Prices are subject to change without prior notice.

≪亞太漫畫系列≫

嫦娥奔月

繪畫：陸少康
翻譯：許國強

亞太圖書有限公司出版